©ME Ink

This Book Belongs To:

Mrs. Callaway

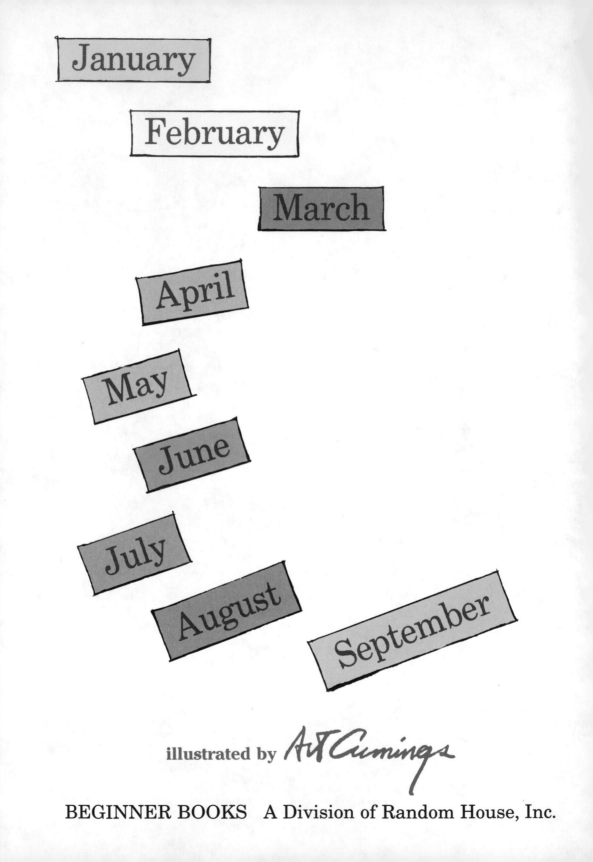

January

February

March

April

May

June

July

August

September

illustrated by *Art Cummings*

BEGINNER BOOKS A Division of Random House, Inc.

www.seussville.com

Library of Congress Cataloging-in-Publication Data:
Seuss, Dr.   Please try to remember the first of Octember!   "B63."
SUMMARY: Every wish is fulfilled on the First of Octember.
[1. Wishes—Fiction.   2. Stories in rhyme]   I. Cumings, Art.   II. Title.
PZ8.3.G276P1   [E]   77-4504
ISBN: 0-394-83563-8 (trade) ; ISBN: 0-394-93563-2 (lib. bdg.)

Printed in the United States of America   15 14 13 12 11 10

BEGINNER BOOKS, RANDOM HOUSE, and the Random House colophon are registered
trademarks of Random House, Inc.

Everyone wants
a big green kangaroo.

Maybe, perhaps,
you would like
to have TWO.

I want you to have them.
I'll buy them for you . . .

. . . if you'll wait
till the First of October.

Everyone wants

a new skateboard TV.

Some people want two.

And some people want three.

Perhaps you want four?

Well, that's O.K. with me . . .

. . . if you'll wait

till the First of Octember.

Just say what you want.
You want pickles on trees?

Want to swing
through the air
on a flying trapeze?

Just say what you want,
and whatever you say,
you'll get
on Octember the First.

WHAT A DAY!

When October comes round,
you can play a hot tune
on your very expensive
new Jook-a-ma-Zoon!

I wish you could play it
in May or in June.

But May is too early.

And June is too soon.

When October gets here,
no work! And no school!

We'll build you a playhouse!
We'll build you a pool!
We would build them
right now,
but right now
is too cool.

And we'll buy you
a wonderful
Jeep-a-Fly kite!

We will!
If you'll wait
till the month is just right.

Octber's the best
because March is too dusty.
And April won't do
because April's too gusty.

What <u>more</u> do you want?

Do you and your dog
want more time to relax? . . .
Less time on your feet
and more time on your backs? . . .
More time in the air
and less time on the ground? . . .

You'll get it
as soon as
Octember comes round.

Want to take a great trip?
Well, I know a great ship!

It sails
to Alaska,
Nebraska and Sweden,
making stops
in Ga-Dopps
and the Garden of Eden.

And it sails on the First of Octember!

What <u>else</u> do you want?

Want to play a new sport?

In Octember
we'll build you
a Hock-Zocker court!

You'll get all that you want.

You just write out your list.

<u>Everyone</u> has an October First list.

Write slowly now!
Don't break your wrist.

Then one of these days
the October First van
will drive up to your house
just as fast as it can.

Whatever you want,

you will get in big bags,

and boxes and crates

with your name on the tags.

You'll have
rockets to shoot.

You'll have
bombs you can burst . . .

On the First of Octember
you'll stay up all night,
drinking 66 six-packs
of Doodle Delight.

Whatever
you ask for,
I want
you to get.

But October—
I'm sorry—
just isn't <u>here</u> yet.

SO . . .

Be sure

to be here.

Be sure you're in town

on Octember the First . . .

. . . when
the
money
comes
down!

It doesn't
come down much
in March
or November—
or even September . . .

. . . or in August,

October,

July

or December.

But
EVERYTHING'S
YOURS . . .

. . . on the First
of Octember!

On the First
of Octember?

Thank <u>you</u>!
I'll remember.

DR. SEUSS (who was known as Theodor Geisel when he wasn't writing or drawing) wrote and illustrated 44 books for children and their lucky parents. But sometimes Dr. Seuss liked to write books and have someone else draw the pictures. For those books he used the pen name Theo. LeSieg (which is Geisel spelled backward!). To draw the pictures for this book, he chose…

ART CUMINGS, who was a cartoonist and magazine illustrator for many years. When his three sons were young, Mr. Cumings decided to start illustrating books for children. He especially enjoyed working on this book since it gave him the chance to work with one of his favorite writers.